Myles,

Happy 1ST Birthday!

With the love and support of the BIG family you have, - You CAN Do ANYTHING

Love,
Grammie : Boppie

YOU CAN!

WORDS OF WISDOM FROM
The Little Engine That Could®

GROSSET & DUNLAP
Penguin Young Readers Group
An Imprint of Penguin Random House LLC

Library of Congress Cataloging-in-Publication Data is available.

ISBN 9781524784683   10 9 8 7 6 5 4

YOU CAN!

WORDS OF WISDOM FROM
The Little Engine That Could®

by Charlie Hart

illustrated by Jill Howarth

inspired by the original book retold by Watty Piper
with illustrations by George and Doris Hauman

Grosset & Dunlap
An Imprint of Penguin Random House

Wake up ready for an adventure.

Always run on time.

Keep yourself in good working order. Everybody needs a little downtime for maintenance.

Life is all about balance.

Remember that some carry loads
that are heavier than yours.
Be patient!

Knowing which track to choose
can be scary.

But nothing feels better than
finally getting started!

If you don't like the direction
you're headed, you can
always change tracks.

Often, the track less taken has an unexpected surprise.

Give free rides.

Being of service to others
means you'll always have plenty
of friends along the way.

You can't always see
where the journey ends when
you're just starting out.

There may be obstacles
you didn't anticipate.

But that doesn't mean there's
not another track to take.

Or a more direct route!

Remember that it's always
darkest before the dawn.

There's always a light at
the end of the tunnel!

Don't forget that everyone travels
on their own track.

Go at your own pace!

Remember, you can always
ask for help.

Working together makes
any job easier.

Don't let a little bad weather
stop you!

Never forget where you came from.

It's okay to take a break.

Remember to take a look around
along the way!

Leave time for fun and games.

A positive attitude always helps
when the going gets tough.

Having many kinds of friends
leads to many kinds of fun!

Sometimes we all need a little push.

Where you've been is just as
important as where you'll go.

You can achieve anything
you set your mind to.

Each new track is an opportunity.

If you think you can . . .

. . . you can!